The Chronicles of William Wilder

Tempura's Treasure

By Sean Conway

The Chronicles of William Wilder
Tempura's Treasure
© Sean Conway 2020 - SeanConway.com

First published in 2020

Mortimer Lion Publishing

www.MortimerLion.co.uk

Chapters

'We were meant to explore this earth like children do, unhindered by fear, propelled by curiosity and a sense of discovery. Allow yourself to see the world through new eyes and know there are amazing adventures here for you.'

Laurel Bleadon Maffei

Chapter 1
The Boy and his Dog

'Hurry up Shackleton, come on. We've got big business today,' I said in my usual morning excitement for the day ahead.

Shackleton looked at me with the same undying love that he always had, then jumped out of his basket, drank from his bowl and came running over to me. He always enjoyed his early morning drink from his bowl because I put some milk left over from my cereal in it for him. It was usually a bit sweet too, with some sugar that hadn't quite dissolved. Shackleton is a beautiful Irish Terrier, golden brown with a long flowing beard that blows in the wind and always get covered in the morning milk which then goes all over my face when he comes to lick me. I don't really like being licked in the face, but I know Shackleton likes it, so I let him. He was named after some famous explorer who went to the South Pole. Father says that's where polar bears and penguins live. I'd like to see a polar bear one day. Father said he wanted a dog that reminded us of home. Mother and Father came over on the big ship from Galway on an island called Ireland over the big sea. He said it had something to do with bad potatoes or something, so he had to come here to start a new life for us. This was before I was born of course, so I didn't experience these bad potatoes he talks about. I don't know what he means by that because I've never had one bad potato in my life. Even the ones that have gone a bit green and have small things growing on them taste good to me. Father even loves those ones too and always buys them from the potato man down the road. The man always asks him if he's sure he wants those ones and gives him a discount. I guess Father is a good customer. The potatoes in Ireland must have been really bad for him to have to emigrate.

Mother didn't like the green potatoes so much. She would always complain and shout at Father. The shouting was really bad and Shackleton and I would hide in the secret fort I had built under our bed. Eventually one day she was gone. Mother was some sort of precious rock dealer and would always bring home brightly coloured rocks and stones and sell them to people. Father said she went off to find the *Tic-Toc-Rock* so that we could get better potatoes. She always spoke about this *Tic-Toc-Rock*. That was three years ago. It sure must be one grand old adventure if she is still looking. Father says it may take her a lifetime. I can't wait to hear all about it when she returns. I do miss her.

Today was Wednesday, my favourite day of the week because it was market day down by the docks. I loved exploring all the fishing boats and the ships that were getting ready to go out into the big wide ocean. Market day meant that Shackleton and I could do our fish run. Wednesday night, Father would cook fish and potato pie. It was my favourite and I'd always sneak a few bits for Shackleton who always sits patiently at my feet during dinner. We don't really have enough room in the apartment for a dining room table, but we manage just fine, sitting around the stove which Father pulls away from the wall and puts a piece of wood over the top and a tablecloth. 'It's always important to have a proper sit-down dinner my son, always remember to have good manners you hear. Remember where we came from. It's very important. We are the proud Wilder family from Galway, don't forget that.'
He'd always tell me how important our family was in Ireland. I'd heard the story a million times but never complained as I knew Father liked to tell it. Shackleton even seemed to know when he was telling it and he'd sit up straight and listen. Even if he was cleaning his little peanuts, or had a whole fish

from the market in front of him, he still stops everything he's doing for Father's story, every time.

'Oi kiddo, what you fancy today? I got a cod or two bits of tuna,' said the fisherman at the market.
'I think the tuna today please Mister.'
'Coming right up boy, and I'll throw in a bit for Shackleton as usual,' said the fisherman.
'Thank you Mister,' I replied.

Since Father started working with the Italians, everyone is really friendly to us. Even the potato man sometimes doesn't charge us for the potatoes and swaps the green ones for the real big ones. That's usually when Father is with his Italian friends. When he is on his own he always gets the green ones. I don't know what he is doing wrong because Shackleton and I always get free fish on Wednesdays, and we have never had the Italians with us. I put this all down to Shackleton. Without him I feel no one would even notice me.

The tuna was wrapped in newspaper and a little bit for Shackleton was cut off which he always loved. I put the fish in my rucksack and headed down to the fishing boats to explore them. Normally no one is allowed near the dock, but Shackleton and I have discovered a secret path through a drainpipe and into the shipyard. Wednesday is also the day after the fishermen have their big party near the rowdy pub on the other side of the docks. Most of the pubs Father goes to are pretty quiet with only a few other customers. Not the sailor's pub though. It's full of loud music, people dancing, and almost everyone spilling most of their drinks on the floor. I guess fishermen just drink a lot more than the Italians. They also wake up really late on Wednesdays, which means Shackleton and I have the entire shipyard to ourselves to explore. 'Right Shackleton, sit!' I said.

Shackleton always sits on the edge of the harbour wall. He's not allowed to come onto the boats with me. I let him once, but the floor was so slippery he nearly caused himself an injury when he slid across the deck and almost over the edge. I don't know if Shackleton can swim or not, I've never seen him do it so I decided he probably can't. From that day he now sits patiently on the edge while I go and explore the fishing boats.

Before everyone became friendly to us, because of the Italians, Shackleton and I would have to come and scrounge for bits of fish left on the boats. They were usually the small ones they couldn't sell at the market but if you got enough, say twenty or thirty of them, Father could still make his famous fish pie. Even though we didn't need to scrounge for fish anymore,

I still did it anyway because Shackleton still enjoys it. I sometimes spy on him from the boat. He has the biggest smile on his face, his tail wagging ferociously. Then when he sees me it's like he wants to jump in the air but knows he's not allowed to move until I say 'come'. He's always so excited when I give him a bit of fish.

The fisherman must have caught a lot of fish yesterday because I managed to find three big ones, nearly ten inches long, each of them. Whenever I get a big catch like this I always dry out some of the fillets and keep them for next time, in case I don't get any fish, I can give Shackleton a dried one and pretend I've just found it. He acts as if it's the freshest fish he has ever eaten but I know he is just pretending. He's such a clever dog.

On the way back from the docks I would often walk past the school I used to go to. I was there for nine months and made quite a few friends. This was before Father worked for the Italians. As soon as this happened, everyone at school would ignore me, and the teachers wouldn't answer my questions, even when I knew I had the right answer. I enjoyed reading and writing and Father always told me this was the foundation for being smart. Even though I was top of my class I practically became invisible overnight. Father said it's because I was becoming too clever for the school and the teachers were too embarrassed to admit it. Eventually Father took me out of school altogether. So now I teach myself. Every afternoon I go to the library and read anything and everything I can. Shackleton is even allowed inside with me now because Mrs O'Brian the library lady, who also left Ireland because of the bad potatoes, feels sorry for him sitting out in the sun while I study.

'I used to have that exact same dog back home in Cork before we left. I couldn't bring him with so I let him loose on the farm. He was a fighter that dog, so I'm sure he found a good home,' she'd say with a croaking voice and a tear in her left eye. Like Father taught me I'd always offer her my handkerchief, but she always declined and took a tissue out from her sleeve. Mrs O'Brian was probably my only friend in the city nowadays.

'How was your day son?' Father asked as he came home.

'Good thanks. Shackleton and I got us some tuna and then I went to the library. Mrs O'Brian told me maybe I should try and learn a language. I've never thought about it before but I think I want to learn Spanish.'

'Spanish?' Father asked curiously.

'Yes, Spanish. I read a book about Spain, which is in Europe. Ireland is in Europe too. I think I want to go there one day and then maybe go back home too.'

'But this is your home son,' said Father seemingly annoyed.

'I know Father, but I've seen all the amazing potatoes that the potato man sells and I want to take one over to Ireland and plant it, so that they can have good potatoes again.'

'I told you that you were too clever for school my son. I bet the teachers wouldn't have thought of that.'

Even though I knew the reality of my one bag of potatoes not being able to solve the bad potato problem, but the simple naivety of the idea meant that adults usually let me get away with it. I knew Father would never let me learn Spanish on my own, he'd make me learn Italian of course, but with an idea as silly as that meant he was more likely to let me fuel my imagination. It's a survival skill I've managed to master over the years. The truth is that I didn't really want to go to Spain at all. What I really wanted to explore was Peru which is in South America. Books in the library showed vast jungles, deep hidden caves, undiscovered tribes and snakes that could eat me and Shackleton in one gulp. That is where I wanted to go one day and I'd need to learn Spanish to survive. I had no idea how I was going to get there and if they'd even let Shackleton come with me, but I'd cross that bridge when it came.

'OK son. I think Spanish would be a good language to learn. Just don't tell the Italians. I think they might have something to say about that,' he winked and sipped his beer.

The months slowly rolled on by and I began to get a basic grasp of Spanish. The only Spanish person I could find in the area was the security guard outside one of the fancy hotels in town. It was a three hour round trip which I could only do once a week with Shackleton. It was my first proper adventure. I packed my bag with some dried fish and a water bottle.

Juan was a tall man with dark skin. He was sixty years old and had the biggest moustache I'd ever seen. When he smiled he had a full row of gold teeth. Most people were scared of him, which is why he made such a good security guard, but not me or Shackleton. He was now my second friend in the city. 'Ola Senor William. Como etsas?' he'd always greet me as I walked towards him.

'Muy bien, gracias.'

Well done, your pronunciation is perfect today Senor, perfecto,' said Juan with a huge grin.

'Gracias,' I said smugly.

Shackleton and I usually arrived just before 1pm when he was allowed a thirty minute lunch break. We'd spend the first ten minutes practicing all the words, sentences and phrases that he'd given me the week before and then the last twenty minutes learning a whole new bunch.

I was a fast learner and was soon bringing him a few new phrases I had learned by myself.

'Mucho impresive Senor,' he'd always say.

He always offered me half his sandwich but I always declined as I don't think he earned very much money and he was certainly too far from the docks to find free fish every day.

Although I couldn't yet have a full conversation in Spanish, I was learning the important phrases. Juan said that maybe in two years' time I would be ready to go to Spain. This was good enough for me. By then I would be twelve and a half years old and almost a teenager. I'm sure Father would let me take the boat to Peru then.

13

Chapter 2
The Great Shipyard

The big boat taking people across the ocean would always come into the harbour once every month. I never knew where they were going, or where they had come from, but just like the fisherman they all seemed very thirsty and would also disappear to the rowdy pub. Many of them were dressed in officer-looking white uniform and a hat that didn't shield their face from the sun which I thought a bit odd. Why wear a hat at all then?

I used to be too scared to explore the big ship when the sailors were in the pub, but in the past few years I had been on board three times, and all the while Shackleton would sit patiently on the harbour wall. The inside of the ship was made of tunnels, cabins, and a huge engine room. I didn't know what anything did but I just enjoyed the smells and imagining where in the world the big ship was taking people. Maybe Peru. I limited my exploring to no more than an hour or until I heard Shackleton give one bark. This meant someone was coming and I'd need to make a run for it.

The main reason I still kept exploring the big ships - because there wasn't any fish to find for Shackleton - was to try and get into one specific room. Each ship had a room with the word *'Treasury'* written on the door. It was usually located below deck in the bow of the boat. I used to ignore it until I read in a book that the Treasury was the part of the boat where sailors kept all the things they found in far off lands; gold, spices, furniture, pianos, anything that they could bring home and sell to the rich folk to make some money for themselves.

This room was always locked but there was a small porthole just big enough for a ten-year-old to crawl through. It was however three metres up on the bulkhead and there was no way of getting to it without a ladder or something to climb on. I had in the past tried to throw a rope with a bit of wood on the end through the hole, hoping the wood would get stuck and I'd be able to climb up, but the rope was too hard to throw and my aim was terrible. It never worked.

I had no intention of taking anything. I just wanted to see what things from different parts of the world looked like. What did they bring back? Was a piano from Peru the same as one from Ireland? Does gold and silver really shine as brightly as they say? As you can imagine, any ten-year old's imagination can run wild with such adventure and of the idea of hidden treasure. If I ever went to South America, I'd look for treasure and bring it back to Father so that he didn't have to buy the green potatoes anymore. This was my dream. Find the treasure and bring it home. But not steal someone else's treasure. That would only bring bad luck. But if I managed to get into the room I'd know for sure if it was even possible to bring back that sort of treasure of my own. I needed to get into that Treasury. It was a matter of great importance.

For the next three months I tried to climb up to the porthole into the ship's Treasury but each time I failed. I tried stacking boxes but there were never enough to build a big enough table, and the one time I did manage to get close, the boxes collapsed under my weight. It was no hope. The only real way to get in was to get a ladder. But where was I going to get that? I figured I'd probably have to make one out of bits of wood and fishing rope lying around the harbour.

Chapter 3
Larry

For the next week while I waited for the big ship to arrive, I went in search of some big sticks and rope to make the ladder. Within a week I had made a six-foot-long ladder. I was, I guessed, four feet tall and an extra foot with my arms in the air. This was just enough for me to reach the porthole. The problem was that I couldn't just be seen all of a sudden walking around with a ladder you see. People would ask questions. I needed to make a plan. The only viable option that Shackleton and I could come up with was to become a window cleaner. It was the perfect plan. I could walk around our neighbourhood and ask people if they wanted their windows cleaned. I'd soon become known as the window cleaning kid and no one would ever question my ladder.

The thing with most window cleaners is that they probably need to clean many windows every day just to make enough money to survive. This means the overall quality was usually poor. Somehow, they get away with it and customers just accepted that their newly cleaned windows, although still dirty in the corners, were better than before so they used them again. I hated cutting corners as it were. I wanted to wow people. And that's exactly what I did when I got my first job. I had asked about twenty businesses and ten private homes before my first commission, the butcher a few blocks away. I didn't know how much to charge so I asked what he'd pay. It wasn't much, but enough to buy perhaps one big potato for Fathers fish pie the following Wednesday. I spent an hour on his three big windows while Shackleton watched on, barking when I missed a spot. By the end the glass was so clean you could barely see there was glass there at all.

'Wow kiddo, you done good. You want to come back next week to do it again?' said the butcher, smiling from ear to ear.

'Yes Sir. I'll be here,' I replied, feeling a strange sense of pride in my work. And with that, Shackleton and I soon became the best window cleaners in town.

Within two weeks me, Shackleton and my ladder, which had now been given a name of its own: Larry, could walk down the street any time of the day and no one would ask any questions. The plan was working perfectly. We even took the ladder down to the market a few times just to keep up appearances and each time we'd get the same remarks from the fishermen.

'No windows down here kiddo, but my spectacles need a clean,' they laughed.

It was all good humoured of course, and made it easy to keep Larry's real purpose hidden in plain sight.

Chapter 4
The Tempura

The following week the next big ship was due in port, the TEMPURA. It was coming from a place called Havana, which I had never heard of, but it sounded exciting. It was only going to be in the dock for Wednesday morning and due to head back to Havana at around midday. This would give me just enough time to get the morning's fish and then climb aboard and crawl into the Treasury while the sailors overslept in the pub.

On Tuesday night Shackleton and I lay awake waiting for the boom of the *Tempura* to shout its arrival in the port. It came at exactly 10.28pm. My heart started to race and Shackleton jumped up on my bed.
'This is it Shackleton,' I said nervously.
He jumped over and licked my cheek giving the sense that he would look out for me. Tomorrow was going to be a big day for us. Who knew what treasures we may discover that came from Havana.

We barely slept a wink and got up at 6am. Father was

already awake and surprised at our early start. 'Got a big job today then kiddo?' he said.

'Yes Father, the bank wants all their windows cleaned, inside and out, before they open, and then we need to get fish for tonight's fish pie,' I replied.

'Ah yes, about that my boy. I'm sorry but your Father has to go away for a month. There is some business to attend to up north. I've already stocked the fridge and the pantry with everything you should need. Tinned food, some vegetables, cereal and butter. You can always go and get some fish from the market yourself if you want, but there should be enough food for you.'

This was the first time Father had been away for this long without making me stay with Mrs Bradley in apartment sixteen. She was a nasty old lady, she really was. She also hated all animals. The last time I stayed there she threatened to turn Shackleton into mincemeat and feed him to the pigeons if he soiled her carpet. Luckily Shackleton never soils anyone's carpet so I wasn't too worried for him, but nevertheless, I didn't want to ever have to stay there again. Being left alone must mean that Father thinks I am old enough to look after myself. Maybe he'd let me go to South America earlier than when I become a teenager. I had better start doing double Spanish lessons each week with Juan, but that will have to be after we explore the *Tempura*.

Father had already packed his bags and we said our goodbyes, and I promised to keep the apartment tidy for his return. His parting words as he went down the stairs were;

'Now don't do anything silly and keep Shackleton out of trouble ok?'

'Of course Father, we never get into any trouble,' I said making sure to cross my fingers behind my back.

'I know you don't my boy. Stay safe and see you in thirty days,' he replied with a smirk suggesting he knew me too well.

'Yes Father. You stay safe too.'

Father laughed and disappeared down the stairs. I was sad to see him go, but my mind quickly returned to the task at hand - the *Tempura*.

'Come on Shackleton, we need to keep up appearances. We need to clean the bank's windows which should take two hours at least. Then we need to get some fish as usual at the market which will take an hour. That takes up till 10am. That leaves us an hour or so before all the sailors return I think. That's more than enough time to climb into the Treasury.'

Shackleton gave a loud bark and ran in circles a few times. His excitement was infectious.

I packed my bags with enough supplies for the day's outing and a little extra for no other reason than to feel like a real explorer. I took Father's old leather rucksack and filled it with some dried fish, a few bananas, a bottle of water, a compass, some matches, a candle, a notebook, a pen, and a small blanket. I knew it was too much and would make carrying Larry more difficult, but that didn't matter. Today was the day I would find some actual treasure. I was going to become a proper explorer, just like the real Mr Shackleton. The only thing I didn't have was a knife. Father said they were too dangerous. I don't think I will need a knife anyway.

The bank's windows were a lot harder to clean than I had expected and took over two hours in the end. As much as I wanted to just do a quick job, I couldn't bring myself to leave any mucky corners. It's something Father always told me. If you do something, do it properly, or not at all. Also, if I did a poor job then they would suspect something was up. Eventually half an hour behind schedule Shackleton and I ran down to the fish market, dragging Larry behind me as if it were a wheelbarrow without a wheel.

'Morning kiddo. All we got is cod today. Is that OK? said the market seller.

'Of course. That's perfect. Thank you,' I said hastily.
'Still cleaning windows then?'

'Yes Sir. Every morning before library.'

The library eh. I wish I had learned to read.'

'Well maybe one day I can teach you.'

'Oh, it's no use. I'm too old in the grave now son.'
'No you're not, it's easy,'

'OK, well when you stop window cleaning you can come teach me how to read.'

'Yes Sir, but that may be in a while. Shackleton and I are in high demand nowadays.'

'I gather that. I never seen the town's windows looking so clean. I very nearly walked right into the baker's door last week. You done good kiddo. Real good.'

'Thank you Mister.'

'Here you go. Make sure you say hi to your Father for me and don't forget to tell him I give you free fish you hear.'

'Of course I will. Thank you,' I replied.

I packed the fish into my rucksack and wandered back as if I was going home. 100 metres down the road I looked to see if anyone was watching and dashed down to the drainpipe that led into the shipyard.

'Come on Shackleton, hurry up. This is not the time to clean your peanuts.'

I couldn't believe him. Of all the times to have a wash, now wasn't it.

The port was really quiet as we carefully made our way from behind lobster pots to fishing nets. I wore my dark green jumper today as it was the closest to the colour of the moss-covered walls in the harbour and most likely to camouflage me.

We reached the gangway and I dropped Larry on the floor, then took Shackleton up to the bow end of the harbour wall. By the looks of things, there was a small window in the Treasury and with any luck I'd be able to see Shackleton and hopefully hear him bark if anyone came.

'Now Shackleton, sit here. I'll be in there.'

I pointed towards the window and realised for the first time how nervous I was, as my fingers were shaking uncontrollably. Shackleton sat immediately and stared at the window, not moving his gaze at all.

'Good boy. I'll be back shortly.'

I ran back to Larry and crossed the gangway on the deck, turning left to head towards the bow. Many of the ships I had explored over the years were kind of the same; take the door near the bow that has stairs going below. Once below there was usually a passage running across to the other side of the boat. Halfway down was another corridor heading towards the bow. At the end of this corridor it opened out again to an area with a hatch above leading onto the deck. This is the area they'd crane out the treasure I presumed. Then there was a double door with four big locks on it. This was the last bulkhead leading into the Treasury. Either side of the double doors were two portholes, three metres high. They had windows on them but I found them mostly to be open, presumably to allow some air to get in. I reached this room in no time at all, my heart racing and shoulders hurting from the weight of Larry. My immediate thought was to put Larry up and scramble to the window but I stopped. Something was wrong. I could feel a small shudder in the boat. This wasn't normal, normally everything was dead still. I listened to hear if Shackleton was barking. He wasn't, I put an ear up against the cold damp hull, but still nothing. Maybe it was my nerves.

'Come on William, get on with it,' I could hear Shackleton say to me if he was here.

'Yes boss,' I said out loud.

I put Larry up against the bulkhead careful not to make a clanging sound. Luckily, he had some rags taped to his top ends to avoid me scratching people's windows when I cleaned them, this provided me with a soft landing when he eventually made contact with the steel of the boat.

This was it, a month of preparation and almost every window in the entire town cleaned to get to this point. I wasn't going to back down now.

Chapter 5

Where is all the Treasure?

I slowly made my way up Larry, being careful that I didn't jolt him. I had nailed bits of old bicycle tyres to his legs for extra grip, however the painted floor which was a little damp was still a death trap. If the bottom gave way something was sure to break - either one of my bones or Larry himself. I needed to be extremely careful.

I got to the top of Larry and stopped to listen for any barking, but there was nothing. I slowly reached up to the window. I stretched out one arm as far as it would go and grabbed the bottom of the porthole. It felt cold and sent shivers down my spine. With a good grip I then stopped holding Larry. The next goal was to take my backpack off and push it through the hole. I slowly slipped if off and raised it above my head by sliding it up the bulkhead next to me. I then pushed it through the window. It disappeared and fell to the ground with an almighty clang on the other side. I froze and listened for Shackleton to bark. Nothing.

I was past the point of no return now. My rucksack was on the other side and at the very least I needed to go and retrieve it. I put both hands on the window and pulled myself up and in the process purposefully pushed Larry over so that he wasn't up against the bulkhead anymore. A ladder lying on the floor is far less conspicuous than one leading up to a porthole window.

Carrying Larry around for a month had given my arms strength I'd never known before, and I found it easy to pull myself up and put my head through the window. Once through I couldn't see anything. It was almost pitch dark apart from the light from the side porthole. I wanted to let my eyes adjust, but all I could think of was having my legs tugged by one of the sailors who had managed to slip past Shackleton. I needed to get inside, I slid even further through the window until my head was now completely upside down. I reached back up with my arms and grabbed the bottom of the window again. My face was against the bulkhead. The idea now was to bring my legs through and then flick them over my head and do a sort of summersault. The plan worked perfectly and before I knew it I was hanging from the window. I let go. The wind rushed past my ears for what seemed like a lifetime, before my feet landed safely on the wooden floor.

I was in. I scrambled around looking for my rucksack in the dark.

'Found it,' I whispered and picked it up. I took it over to the window for some light to get my candle lit. I peered out to see if Shackleton was there. He immediately saw me and his tail started to wag. I could sense his excitement. I waved and he looked from left to right but didn't bark. I knew I was in safe hands with him on guard.

Slowly I found my candle and matches. My eyes, now accustomed to the bright outside after looking through the window, sent the entire room into darkness again. As soon as my candle was lit however, I'd find my treasure. I struck the first match and slowly brought it to the candle, it took instantly and soon there was a warm glow all over the Treasury. I moved the candle away from my face to shine a light into the room. My heart sank. It was almost empty. There was no treasure at all, none. Besides a small leather case right in the far corner, and a pile of small rocks, which I guessed to be ballast for the ship, the entire room was bare. How was this possible? I sat down on the cold floor feeling deflated. Maybe this treasure hunting wasn't all it was made out to be. Then I heard Shackleton bark. That was the signal people were coming. I jumped up and ran to the window. His tail wasn't wagging anymore. He waited a bit and then gave another bark. I needed to get out of there.

I fumbled with my rucksack and then looked up at the porthole. My heart jumped. In my planning I imagined a room full of antiques and boxes of treasure and getting out was never going to be an issue, as I would have been able to pile everything high up and climb back out the window. I paced around the room looking for something, anything that I may stand on to help me reach the window. There was nothing. Maybe I could run and jump up. I went as far as I could into the bow and ran right for the bulkhead and leaped into the air as high as I could. My body and face slammed into the cold steel and I bounced off and back onto the floor. A sharp pain shot down my arm. It was my shoulder. I tried to lift my arm in the air but the pain was too strong. I slumped back against the hull. Shackleton barked again and I looked out at him. We caught each other's eyes and I could see the panic in his face and he could see mine. Then a jolt. The bow slowly started to move away from the harbour wall. But I couldn't hear the engines. How is it we were moving? Then another jolt and we moved away even further. Shackleton didn't move, we just stared at each other while he barked every twenty seconds or so like I'd taught him so well. The ship was being pulled away from the wall by a tug boat. The tug would take us out of the harbour and then we'd set sail.

My heart raced. I needed to get off this ship. I figured I had another ten minutes before the ship was in open sea where I could still jump off and swim to shore. After that it would be too dangerous. The engine then started up and I could hear people coming down the corridor. Do I shout for help? No. Who knows what trouble I may land up in if they found me.

'What's this ladder doing here Bill?' I heard someone say outside the door.

'Dunno, must have been one of the cleaners who left it I guess.'

'A real short cleaner looks like.'

They both burst out laughing.

'Do we need to check the Treasury?'

'Na, there's nothing in there except Captain's special suitcase.'

'Oh yeah his *special suitcase*. What does he keep in there?

'I don't know but the rumour is that it has some treasure map for the mountains around Viñales.'

'I've heard that rumour before but there's no treasure up there anymore. He's the fifth Captain of the

Tempura who's gone looking for the treasure and come back empty handed. The last one came back with that pile of rocks, and he mysteriously disappeared before reaching port. Fell overboard I guess.'

'I know. He's a bit crazy old Capt.'

'You can say that again.'

And their voices disappeared down the corridor and out of earshot.

My intrigue for Captain's treasure map wasn't nearly as strong as my desire to get out of the Treasury, and all thoughts of exploration were soon gone while I tried over and over again to climb up to the porthole. Between each failed attempt I'd go to the window and I'd see Shackleton still sitting there staring at me. It was heart-breaking. All I wanted to do was tell him I would be OK. The bow was about fifty metres from the harbour wall while the stern seemed to still be attached as we swung round. I gave another leap for the window and fell back down again, this time really hurting my shoulder. I hobbled back to the side window to see Shackleton, but he was gone.

'Shackleton,' I shouted in a whisper.

I hope he hadn't tried to swim to me. He couldn't swim. I scoured the harbour wall but couldn't see him.

Then the engines turned over again and the whole ship started to vibrate. We had obviously left the harbour wall now and were heading straight for the open sea. All I could think about was Shackleton, now wondering the streets trying to see if I had made it off, or even worse, trying to swim after me. He'd be stranded and have no way of getting back into the apartment. Mrs Bradley would make certain of that I'm sure. I looked out of the window again. Shackleton was nowhere to be seen and we were now at least 100 metres from where the *Tempura* had docked.

A few minutes later while I rested from yet another failed attempt at reaching the porthole, the ship started to rise and fall. We were now outside the harbour wall and into the big swell of the Atlantic Ocean. It was over. I was stuck on this ship till it docked again, in Havana. I sank to the floor, tired and in pain. This was not the way things were meant to have worked out.

Chapter 6
The Treasure Map

Over the next few hours I did nothing more than sit in the corner trying to come to terms with my new situation. I was on a ship, going to a place called Havana, without Shackleton. Father wouldn't know I was gone until he returned in a month and even then, there would be no trace of me. I could of course surrender by knocking on the inside of the door and crying for help, but I feared this would land me in even more trouble.

My attention then turned to the Captain's suitcase still hidden in the shadows of the bow corner and I remembered what I heard from the sailor. A map they said. My mind wondered. I shuffled over to inspect the case. It was an old case. Far older than maybe Father by the looks of the worn corners. Considering the case was so highly valuable to the Captain, it surprised me to find it had no lock on it. I unclicked the two latches and opened it slowly. The case's inside was lined with old newspapers stuck on with glue. They were from the First World War it seemed. This must be a very old suitcase indeed. There was a pen, some writing paper, and a notebook which didn't have any drawings of maps except day to day occurrences on board the *Tempura*. Then I saw it, the map. It was rolled up and tied together with a bit of old bark from a tree. I untied the knot and opened the map out. It was hard to see in the light so I moved it over to the window. It was a map of the Viñales area as it said written across the top in calligraphy writing. There was a mountain range in the north and a few hills dotted around. On one of the hills lay the word 'cave' and next to it in red ink it simply said: TREASURE TIME. I had no idea if Viñales was anywhere near Havana, but if it was I needed to go and find out what *Treasure Time* meant. I took out my notebook and copied the map down exactly. On the back of the map there was a riddle too.

Where treasure lies there are no stairs
High above what comes in pairs
The darkest void lies in plain sight
But danger lurks when day turns night
Dalmatian spots echo before
The whistling birds you must not ignore
If a man does be caught to steal
His digits left, up two, and kneel

Of the three there can only be one
When dusk does glow the wolves become
It's in the jaws you shall go
And here lies the treasure for all who know

It took me no more than five minutes to copy the map when I heard someone coming down the corridor.

'Yes Captain, the case is still there. I checked it in last night and the door has been locked ever since and only you have the key.'

'Wonderful,' I heard the old man say. He had an English accent.

I heard the first of the locks being opened. I ran back to the case, rolled the map up, tied it together and put it back. I couldn't remember where everything was but I figured it didn't matter. I closed the case when I heard the final lock being opened.

Now what? I thought. Hide in the dark corners. I ran to the port side corner where the pile of rocks were. The door swung open and I was blinded by the light from outside. I knew the Captain's eyes would take time to adjust. He walked into the room directly for his case, then he stopped. He looked at the case and momentarily around the room. He was a scary looking man with a very unshaven face, scruffy white hair and a dirty jacket that didn't quite fit around his huge overhanging belly. He walked with a slight limp too. I held my breath even longer and it felt like my eyes were going to pop out. The Captain looked into my corner and we made eye contact. I thought it was all over, he'd surely seen me. I held my breath. We stared at each other but his eyes must not have adjusted to the dark yet, so he slowly turned away and walked over to his case, picked it up and walked out again. This time leaving the door wide open.

'Don't bother locking it boys. Smells rotten in there. It needs an airing out.'

Then I heard his footsteps disappear down the corridor. This was my time to escape.

I waited a few minutes before getting up. As I stood up I dislodged some of the rocks. A few came crashing to the floor with the loudest bang. I froze and tucked my head down near the rocks again. I waited and waited but no one came back. I was just about to get up when something caught my eye. One of the rocks, about the size of a baseball, was almost perfectly round and had a meandering green line running around its entire circumference. It looked very precious indeed.

'Mother would love this,' I said in a whisper. I could give it to her as a welcome back gift when she returns. I picked it up and was surprised how heavy it was. Far heavier than any other rock of its size. Three times as heavy.

'This must be a very precious rock,' I said again and put it in my rucksack.

I then stuck my head out of the door. The coast was clear. I needed to make a run for it, to the deck. By chance we may be near enough to the coast for me to jump and swim for it. I ran back down the main corridor to the bit where I could go left or right and back up onto deck. I turned right and ran to the stairs. I had just put my foot on the first rung when I heard a very familiar sound. A bark. It couldn't be? It was coming from the end of the corridor running down the side of the engine room. I listened again. Another bark. It sounded exactly like Shackleton. I stepped down from the stair and slowly tiptoed towards the door which was fifteen metres away. The engine slowly chugging away to my left would have drowned out any footsteps in any case, but I was trying to be cautious. I reached the door and opened it slowly. What hit me first was the distinct smell of animals. Then the sounds. The bark again, then a squawk, a gurgle and a coo. I looked up. In front of me was a wall of cages from the floor to the deck above, five metres or so high, and in each cage was an animal. Mostly exotics ones; parrots, tortoises, a monkey and even two pigs, a sheep and loads of rabbits which I presumed were for eating. Then I heard the bark again. I looked off to my left into the far corner of the room, my eyes adjusting slowly. The bark came again.

'Shackleton?' I said softly.

He barked again. I knew it was him. I ran over and he jumped up. I pressed my face up against the cage.

'Shackleton, it's you, it's really you. How did you get on the boat? You silly boy.'

Shackleton licked me all over my face. We were reunited.

'Let's get you out of here,' I said and Shackleton sat down and looked sad. I went to the door and tried to open it but it was locked.

'Right Shackleton, don't you worry, I'll get you out of here I promise,' I said.

'Who are you?' A beaming voice echoed through the door. I turned around to see one of the sailors' silhouette taking up the entire frame.

'I'm, well. . . . '

He didn't let me finish.

'Come here boy. This is not a place for you. Let me take you back to your parents. Come.'

He walked over and grabbed my arms. Shackleton barked and the sailor banged his fist on the cage.

'Shut up mutt. Be quiet. Stupid harbour dogs. We don't get much for them on the black market but he looks like a purebred so he may fetch something for us in Havana; enough for a round of rum in the tavern for the lads anyway. If not, we'll just shoot the bugger and feed him to the pigs,' said the man almost excited by the idea.

I was stunned into silence. He can't shoot Shackleton. He just can't. Not my best friend. Before I could even protest he dragged me out the room, down the corridor, up the stairs and along the deck. The sun blinded me instantly. Ten metres ahead was another door, not a steel door like the ones below, but a beautifully crafted wooden door with thick windows.

We went through the door and into what looked like a very fancy dining room.

'Now son, which are your parents?'

The room went silent as everyone turned to look at me. There were about fifteen people in the room, possibly only five couples who could potentially be my parents.

'Speak up boy,' he shouted. I could sense his anger.

'Come on, whose child is this?' he shouted again.

No one would claim me. Of course not. My fate was surely sealed.

'Right then, maybe it's one of the servants who brought you here.'

He grappled my injured shoulder and whipped me around. A shaft of pain shot down my arm, I tried to hide it but I let out a squeal. I feared this was not going to end well for me. Maybe I too would land up in a cage to be sold off.

Chapter 7
Mr Ernie

'Jerry, sorry. The boy is mine,' I heard from behind me. The angry sailor man turned around with a questioning expression on his face.

'Ernie, is this boy yours?'

'Yes Jerry, he's my nephew. He's coming to help me in the house while I write.'

'What you writing now Ernie?'

'You know I can't tell you Jerry. Now come here boy. You had me worried. Where have you been? Don't tell your mother. She'll never let you come with me again.'

Jerry let go my arm and I walked over to the man sitting by himself at the table. He was an elderly man, about fifty years old I guessed, but it's hard for any ten-year-old child to guess how old people really are. In any case, anything older than thirty is ancient. He wore a linen shirt, blue trousers and shoes you might see people on yachts wearing. Not the sailors, but the fancy folk down by the part of the dock where the private yachts are kept. I used to go there every now and again with Shackleton but found it a bit boring. I much preferred the fishing trawlers' docks.

'Thanks Jerry. He's fine now.'

The old man kicked the chair opposite him with his foot. I took my rucksack off and sat down. He whispered to me.

'What's your name son? In case I have to call you. They need to believe our story.'

'William Wilder, Sir.'

'Well isn't that a wonderful name. William Wilder. It sounds very grand. I think you'll be a fabulous explorer one day.'

'Thank you, Sir.'

'My name is Ernest, but you can call me Ernie.'

Hello Mr Ernie.' I put my hand out to shake his.

'How very polite William Wilder. You've been taught well.'

'Thank you, Sir.'

'So tell me, why are you on this ship? By the look on your face I knew you were not meant to be here. That's why I helped you.'

'Well Mister, I kind of got stuck exploring when the boat was in the docks, and didn't get off in time, now Shackleton and I are stuck here, going far, far away I think.'

'Shackleton, who is Shackleton?'

It's my dog Mister. He's been taken and they have him in a cage. If they can't sell him they are going to shoot him.'

'Well we can't have that now can we. I'll see what I can do. Don't worry William. Have some food. Would you like mussels or crab?'

I had never had either of those before. I wondered if mussels gave you actual muscles.

'The mussels please Sir.'

'Good choice.'

Mr Ernie called the waiter over and ordered us both a plate of mussels with steamed vegetables on the side.

'So why are you on the boat Mr Ernie?' I eventually asked after finishing my bowl of mussels. They were almost the best thing I'd ever eaten. Almost as good as Father's fish pie. Maybe a few potatoes with the mussels would have made them better I thought.

'Well William. I am a writer and I moved to Cuba a few years ago. It feels freer for my thoughts to run wild.'

'So you write books?'

'Yes, novels.'

'What are they about?' I asked inquisitively.

'Well whatever takes my fancy, wherever I choose to let my mind wander. It's a wonderful thing being an author.'

'So what are you writing now then?'

'Well truthfully, I'm just finishing of my latest book.' And then he leaned in and whispered in my ear.

'Don't tell anyone, but I don't think this book is any good. I'm desperate for a new idea. What do you think I should write about?' he asked.

'I don't know. I will have a think,' I said, before returning to the subject we brushed over - Cuba.

'So this ship is heading for a place called Cuba?'

'Wow kiddo. You don't even know where you were going?'

'Well, I thought we were going to Havana.'

'Havana is in Cuba, it's the capital city.'

'Oh,' I said feeling embarrassed for not knowing.

'When does the ship head back home from Havana?'

'It usually returns once a month. So, you're stuck in Cuba for a month. Should we telegram your parents to let them know?'

'Well, Mother has gone to find the *Tic-Tok-Rock* and has been away for three years now and Father is on a business trip up north with the Italians for a month, so there would be no one to telegram. No one will miss me being away. Only Shackleton, but he is here on the ship with me in any case.'

'What about school? They will miss you surely.'

Ernie looked worried for me.

'Well, I had to leave school too because as soon as Father started working for the Italians, the teachers and kids started to ignore me. So eventually I left. Also I think I was too clever for the teachers anyway, that's what Father says.'

'I believe it too. Any boy who manages to find a way onto a ship like this must be very clever indeed.'

'Thank you Mister. I've been teaching myself in the library with Mrs O'Brian.'

'Good on you.'

Just then a waiter came over and asked Mr Ernie in Spanish if I would like a glass of lemonade. Before he could answer on my behalf I replied, in perfect Spanish.

'Si Senor. Muchas gracias.'

Mr Ernie looked surprised.

'You speak Spanish then?'

'Well, kind of. I've been learning in the library and with Juan, the security guard in town who has been teaching me as well. I want to explore Peru one day so that's why I learned. I told Father it's because I want to visit Spain, which is sort of near Ireland, to take them some better potatoes. But the truth is I want to go to Peru.'

'Well, you really are a clever clogs aren't you William Wilder?'

Mr Ernie laughed with a deep warm breath. I decided we were going to be friends.

'Well, how good is your spelling William? You will be in Cuba for a month and I could do with someone to spell check what I write, and also someone to help me translate. My Spanish is *poco* alright, but if you were there translating for me, I would find that ever so useful. I can pay you too. That way you can afford the ship back home in a month.

'Ok Mr Ernie. It's a deal.'

I put out my hand and we shook on it. My mind then turned back to the Captain's map.

'Mr Ernie. Is Viñales in Cuba too?'

'Why, yes it is. It's the most beautiful part, 100 miles west of Havana. It takes a few days on horse and cart to get there but it's worth the trip. Maybe we'll go one day. How come you've heard of it?'

I blushed. I liked Mr Ernie but I didn't want to give away my secret map.

'Oh I read it in a book about jungles once,' I lied and felt guilty for doing so.

'Well there are jungles there for sure, vast and very dense ones. If you ever wanted to hide away from the world, that's where you would go.'

We sat in silence for the rest of the meal. I dreamed about the treasure map while Mr Ernie looked around the room and jotted down notes when something interesting happened. A man knocked a glass of wine all over his wife's dress. He then stood up and when he leaned over to wipe her, his tie fell into his soup. I guess being a writer involves observing people, in case you want to write about it someday. I think I'd be a good writer. Most people would ignore a ten-year-old boy, unless Shackleton is with me, then we get a lot of attention. I guess if I wanted to be a writer I'd have to leave Shackleton at home. I couldn't do that. Maybe being a writer wasn't for me then.

After lunch Mr Ernie said he was heading off for a nap and I could go on deck and relax. I said my thank yous and he disappeared off down the corridor. I wanted to go on deck to explore, as I hadn't done any of that in the past, mainly because I would have been seen. But before that I wanted to go back and see Shackleton. I secretly snuck a few mussels in my pocket when Mr Ernie wasn't looking. I bet Shackleton was starving.

I crept back down below and slipped into the animal room to the squawks of parrots and stench of poo. Shackleton barked.

'Shhh Shackleton. We need to keep quiet. I have a plan to get you out.'

Shackleton sat down like he would do every time I asked.

'Here you go. It's not much but I bet tastes good.'

I handed him the mussels and he wolfed them down. I then gave him my palm to lick the juices off. He seemed in good spirits for a dog in a cage surrounded by many creatures I'd only ever shown him in books from the library.

'Now be a good boy when I'm gone you hear. There are some nasty people on this boat.'

I left Shackleton curled up in the corner and went back up to the top deck to survey our position.

We had been at sea for quite some time, and I saw that we were heading south, following the coast. The shore was maybe five miles off to my right, only just visible and certainly too far to swim. Even if Shackleton wasn't on board I don't think I would have risked it. I found a quiet shelter out of the wind and opened my backpack. I took out my notebook and opened it to the map. It looked exactly as I had remembered it from the Captain's version. I felt pleased with my drawing skills. I looked at it closer.

Viñales was two days from Havana and the map showed an area that was thirty miles wide. It didn't say how wide on the north-south line it was, but I guessed it to be maybe twenty miles. The mountain I was looking for, the one where *Treasure Time* was written, was right up on the top left corner of the map. As the crow flies it was about twenty-five miles from Viñales, no doubt more in real life. If I worked for Mr Ernie for ten days that would give me enough money to maybe catch a lift or something. Two days to get there, plus the two days back, that would mean I'd have a week or so to try and find the treasure. That was my plan, but not before I made sure Shackleton would be set free.

That evening Mr Ernie came back downstairs and we ate together. He handed me three pages of writing.
'Here you go William. This is what I wrote this morning. Let me know what you think.'
'Yes Sir,' I said excitedly.
I'd never met a real author before. I was intrigued as to what they would write about and what a manuscript looked like.
'The first manuscript is always rubbish.' Mr Ernie laughed and called the waiter, ordering a whisky for himself and a lemonade for me.

I checked over his writing while we ate and jotted down some of my ideas in pencil in the margins.

After my edits, I thought it a good time to revisit the subject of Shackleton.

'Mr Ernie. You mentioned yesterday about Shackleton. You said I shouldn't worry, but I do worry. He's down there, all alone with the other animals and who knows when he's been fed or watered. Also, he has nowhere to do his, you know, business.'

Ernie looked up with a questioning eye.

'You really do love that dog don't you?'

'Yes Mr Ernie. Besides Mrs O'Brian and Juan, Shackleton is my only friend.

'OK, well a man cannot be without his partner in crime now can he?'

Ernie signalled for the waiter to come over.

'Send for the Captain old boy,' he boomed across the dining room before the waiter was anywhere near our table.

'Si Senor,' the waiter replied and hurried himself away.

Five minutes later the Captain came through the door. He looked at me, and for a moment I thought he'd recognise me from the Treasury but his gaze soon went to Mr Ernie.

'Ah, Ernie. Good to have you on board again. I hope things went well with the publishers then?'

'So, so. It'll be a month before I hear anything. Anyway, what about you Captain? How is your daughter?' replied Mr Ernie.

'She doing OK. Been in the hospital for months now, we're just waiting on the operation you see. If we don't get it then I fear the worst,' he said and then quickly changed the subject.

I wasn't sure if he was telling the truth. He had a look on his face that suggested he was lying. Maybe for sympathy or something. People often tell tall tales of sorrow when they are trying to divert your attention away from what they are really up to. Something told me that the Captain was up to no good.

'What can I do for you then?' he continued.

'Well Captain. A little birdie tells me you have a hound below deck.'

'Ah yes, a harbour mongrel we found before leaving.'

'Well, I'd like to purchase that hound from you.'

'The hound. Whatever do you want with a hound?'

'I need a rat catcher back home. I tried a cat, but the damn thing is scared to death of rats and hasn't caught one. I need a dog I think. That one looks better than the standard short legged hounds of Havana. He looks like an athlete.'

'Well it's a fine hound it is, a real gem. He'll fetch top dollar at the market.'

'I'm sure he will. What will he fetch right here right now?'

The Captain took his gaze off Mr Ernie and looked at the ceiling light covered in moths for second.

'Ten Dollars, and that's a bargain,' he finally said.

Mr Ernie replied straight away.

'Five Dollars and I name a character in my next book after you.'

The Captain thought for moment.

'Only if you promise not to kill him off in the first chapter.'

'Deal, and only if you let the hound loose right away and let him join us.'

'Well he seems a good-tempered hound so we have a deal Sir.'

They both put a hand out and shook. Then Captain turned around, summoned one of the waiters and told him to go and get Shackleton. I couldn't believe it. Mr Ernie had saved Shackleton. I was indebted to him. Moments later Shackleton bounded through the doors and ran right up to me and sat down.

'Wow, kiddo, that dog seems to like you,' the Captain said, acknowledging me for the first time.

'I have a way with dogs Sir,' I said, trying not to give anything way.

'Yes you do. It also seems you have a good eye for shoes. My daughter has the same ones. They have an anchor on the soles don't they?'

The Captain was noticing my brown leather shoes. Father had bought them for me down by the market. I thought they were a bit girly, but he said they were made for boys and girls. I did like them though.

'Yes Sir,' I said, still too terrified to look him in the eye.

'They leave an anchor mark on the sand when I walk.'

'I know. That's why I bought them for my daughter so I can always find her if she walks off.'

I wondered if Father bought them for me for the same reason.

'Right, best be off. Storm approaching. Nothing serious but try to sleep against the wall tonight Ernie, so that you don't fall off your bunk again.'

The Captain left and Mr Ernie sat in silence, staring at Shackleton as I fed him some of my scraps and put some lemonade in a cup for him.

'He is a beautiful hound,' he eventually said.

'What kind is he?'

'An Irish Terrier. One day I want to grow a big ginger beard just like he has.'

'And what a mighty beard it shall be Master William.

'How many days to Havana?' I asked.

I had been putting off the question in fear that it would take two weeks or more. If that happened I'd have no time to make my way to Viñales, so it was a welcome surprise to hear it was only three days and two nights before we would reach Havana.

That night Mr Ernie put Shackleton and I into our very own cabin. Shackleton could stay with me as long as he didn't sleep on the bed. He never slept on the bed anyway and was quite happy curled up in the corner by the door; my very own guard dog. I always make sure he's asleep before me. I know when this happens because he starts snoring and his beard moves in and out with his breath. Soon after I was fast asleep too.

The two nights and three days passed very quickly as I spent the mornings checking over Mr Ernie's writing and adding my notes. He'd only come down to breakfast at around 11am. He said he does his writing in the morning and his thinking in the afternoon. His thinking time also happened to be his drinking time it seemed. Whisky is what he liked the most. I wondered if whisky helps your thinking. Adults I came to realise are just a bit different from kids and have their own rules. I kind of hoped that I would never become an adult. Life with Shackleton - although currently we were in a bit of a pickle - was simple, and I liked it that way.

On the evening of the third day the Captain came into the dining room and announced we were soon to be reaching Havana. My heart raced. I thought it would be years before I'd be exploring far off lands. Shackleton and I weren't just exploring now, we were treasure hunters.

Chapter 8
Havana

It was nearly nightfall when we eventually disembarked.

'Right William, we'll get a taxi from here. It's about one hour and can be a bumpy ride so hold on tight.' There was a rickshaw waiting for us and the driver welcomed Mr Ernie. We made our way south east through the city. It was hard to see the city in the dark but every now and then I caught glimpses of grand pillar fronted buildings and large forts. I couldn't wait to explore the city in the daytime. Shackleton too seemed very interested and spent the entire hour with his nose in the air, taking in all the new smells and hearing all the new sounds.

Mr Ernie lived in a wonderful house just on the outskirts of town. The long drive up the gentle hill brought you up to the front of the house. On the inside it was open planned and ever so big. I think half his lounge was bigger than Father's entire apartment. On almost every wall was the skull of some sort of animal that Mr Ernie had hunted. I didn't really like the idea of hunting, but Mr Ernie insisted the money he spent to hunt the animals was well used to save many more. It didn't make sense to kill one animal just to save another but I guess it's just another silly thing that adults do.

The front of the house opened up to the most spectacular view overlooking Havana. I could see why Mr Ernie chose to live here. You could see the ocean in the far distance with a multitude of brightly coloured buildings sprawling all the way to the foot of Mr Ernie's hilltop house. Off to the side was a sort of turret, or watchtower. Right at the top is where I think he did most of his writing.

Mr Ernie then led me down the corridor to another room at the back of the house.

'Right William, you and Shackleton can sleep in this room. I'll have someone make the beds up for you. Tomorrow we go to the market to buy food. With your Spanish they can't rip me off this time,' he joked and winked at me.

'Yes Sir. Fish markets I know very well.'

'Well that's good then, see you in the morning.'

Shackleton and I slept like logs and awoke as the sun burst through the shutters. It was a glorious day outside and all I wanted to do was explore. However,

I knew I was in Mr Ernie's hands. He was up early too and we shared a cup of tea, a mango and some guava fruit. I'd never had guava before. I liked it because it wasn't as sweet as mango. I tried to give Shackleton a bit but he sniffed at it and turned away in disgust. He hadn't had his bowl of watery milk in days.

'Right kiddo. I have a few more days of writing before I finish this book. I'm heading off to my study now. I'll be back at 10am for you to go over my writings. Your ideas were splendid, just splendid.'
'Yes Mr Ernie,' I said, finishing off my last corner of guava.

I got to see the rest of Mr Ernie's house while he went up to his writing tower. I don't know how he managed to write up there because the view was so spectacular. I'd constantly be looking over Havana all day. No wonder he only ever wrote in the mornings.

His garden was paradise. Tennis court surrounded by a mini bamboo forest. A tropical looking swimming pool with tables and chairs at one end. I wanted to go for a swim, but decided to explore the almond tree forest just below the house instead, because I didn't pack my swimming trunks.

At 10am exactly for the next three days I heard Mr Ernie call for me from his study in the watchtower. Shackleton and I would run up. On the third day Mr Ernie looked a lot more relaxed than the previous days.

'Right kiddo. I have finished this book, finally. As I've said it's not my masterpiece, but I will send it to the publishers on the next ferry. The same ferry you go back on.'

'Well done Mr Ernie. That's great news.'

'It's only great news once I hear what the publishers have to say, but for now, it's done and I can focus some energy on thinking about the next book, and fishing. Do you like fishing?'

'I don't know, I've never tried.'

'Oh well then. Tomorrow we shall take my boat out.'

'Can Shackleton come?'

'Of course he can, as long as he doesn't scare the fish away.'

'He won't Mr Ernie. I promise.'

The following day we went down to the dock, ready to head out to the deep ocean. As we were readying the boat, I noticed the Captain of the *Tempura* loading up a horse and carriage with all manner of boxes, crates, barrels and food.

'What's the Captain doing there?' I asked Mr Ernie.
'Well rumour has it he has found the secret map of Columbus which has the location of a very important cave.
'Really?' I asked nervously.
My heart jumped and Shackleton did a little bark.
'Yes, but it's all nonsense. There is a rumour Columbus hid some very valuable treasure in the mountains around Viñales. However no one has ever seen or heard of this map he claims to have.'
'But what if it is true?'
'Well then good luck to him. If it's true then he may actually become the character in my next novel.'

I couldn't believe it. He was heading to Viñales today or tomorrow. I still had a week with Mr Ernie to earn enough money to pay for my return ferry. With the head start of a week, he'd surely find the treasure before me and I'd never be able to help Father stop working for the Italians and afford better potatoes. It's just not fair, I thought. We needed the treasure more than the Captain did.

I helped Mr Ernie load his boat with the rods, tackle, various forms of bait, and then clambered on board. 'Careful Shackleton. The deck is real slippery. Best you stay on the lower deck,' said Mr Ernie.

I think he was starting to like Shackleton.

Mr Ernie's boat was a small 28-foot cabin cruiser. A cabin at the bow end and an open aired wheelhouse at the stern where you manned the vessel. At the back was one single wooden fishing chair, complete with a cup holder between your legs for the end of the rod and a large footrest to hunker down when you catch a big one. You could also climb up to the roof of the wheelhouse and steer from there if you needed more visibility, or when you needed to dock. She really was a beautiful vessel indeed.

'What are we going to fish for today Mr Ernie?' I asked.

'Barracuda William. We're going for cuda,' he replied with a genuine excitement that you don't often see in adults I thought. Most of the adults I know seem very serious. Mr Ernie wasn't like that at all. Especially after his midday 'thinking' medicine as he liked to call it, which he kept in a hip flask in his jacket pocket.

'A dram a day keeps the doctor away,' he used to say.

'What's a dram?' I asked.

'It's what they call a measure of whisky in Scotland, a dram. It's practically medicine for me. Helps me unwind and see the world through different eyes.'

'What do you mean different eyes?' I asked. I didn't quite understand. I thought we all had the same eyes, even though they were different colour sometimes.

'Well William. Life happens before our eyes, every day. You can choose how you interpret these activities and the things you see. You can choose to believe whatever stories you want to believe. For example, a man staggers up to you and asks for some change. You can decide to interpret that situation in two ways. 1; he's an old drunk and wants money to buy more alcohol, or 2; He's a diabetic and his low sugar levels have made him delirious and he has walked out his house without his wallet and now needs some money to buy some sweets to restore his blood sugar levels. Of course, situation number 1 is far more likely, but if you chose to believe situation number 2, you will lead a happier, more empathetic life.'

I gave it some thought for a moment.

'So I should always give staggering old begging men some money then?' I asked.

'No of course not, they will probably buy alcohol. But you should always give them some candy.'

Mr Ernie burst out laughing and rubbed his belly with one hand. It was all very confusing what Mr Ernie was saying. I guessed I was too young to really understand. Maybe it'd make more sense when I got older.

As we were heading out of the harbour, we passed a small skiff with an old shirtless man sitting at the back paddling slowly out to sea. He looked very interesting. 'What's that man doing?' I asked.

'He's an old fisherman William. He goes out every day in the hope of a big fish. Maybe today will be his lucky day.'

'I hope so too,' I replied.

Fishing for the most part was a lot of sitting down and doing nothing. Mr Ernie had his telescope out and regaled tales from the sea and made up stories about various other boats he saw far off on the horizon. We played a game of: 'where do you think the ship came from?' Mr Ernie would then look through his telescope and tell me the answer by the flag that each ship was flying. It was incredible to see where they were all going; Santiago, Cape of Good

Hope, India and many other places I had never heard of.

Suddenly my line started to wizz.

'You've got one kiddo. Hurry, grab the rod,' shouted Mr Ernie.

I ran over and he helped me with the rod and showed me what to do.

'Pull up hard and then when you let it down, reel as fast as you can. Pull and reel. Pull and reel,' shouted Mr Ernie again.

I did as he said, but it was much harder than it looked.

'You've got a real fighter,' he said.

The rod was getting pulled left and right.

'We must make sure the fish doesn't swim under the boat or the line may get caught in the propeller and break.'

I pulled hard. My muscles were on fire. I could feel the pain in my shoulder from trying to escape the Treasury.

It took half an hour to eventually get the fish on board.

'Well done William Wilder. Your first ever fish; a twelve-pound tuna. Not a *cuda*, but good enough. We shall feast happy tonight.'

The rest of the afternoon I caught four more fish which we kept, and Mr Ernie caught three which he returned back to the ocean saying he didn't need any fish now that I was catching so many. At sunset we returned to the harbour and passed the same old fisherman heading back after his day of fishing.

We pulled up alongside him.

'Got any big ones today?' I asked in my broken Spanish.

He just looked up and shook his lead. He didn't say a word. He didn't need to. The bottom of his skiff had only four medium sized ones. Enough to maybe feed just his family, not enough to sell at the market.

'Can we give him one of our fish Mr Ernie?' I asked

'You can try, but he'll probably decline.'

'Why is that?'

'Well because these old fishermen believe you catch the fish you deserve. If you have caught a bigger fish, it's because you need it more than him.'

'But we don't need it Mr Ernie. We have lots of food.'

'I have lots of food William. You do not. The fish you caught are for you to sell at the market to help pay for your adventures.'

Mr Ernie was right. I had gotten pretty lucky that he had rescued me and was sheltering me for a week. Although the money I earn from Mr Ernie as his translator and spell checker was enough to make my way home, I still needed to get to Viñales and that was of much urgency. So maybe I did need to catch a big fish after all. If I sell it at the market I may have enough to get to Viñales. Maybe the fisherman was right. He on the other hand I guess was content, for now. Maybe one day he'd catch the biggest of all fish. I sure hope he does.

As we came into harbour, men rushed for the boat. 'Pescado Senor, pescado?' They asked holding handfuls of money at us.

'What's happening Mr Ernie?'

'Well William, these are the market sellers. They come to every fishing boat and buy fish so they can sell it in the market. Kind of a middleman between the fisherman and the consumer.'

'Why doesn't the fisherman just sell them himself?'

Well he doesn't have the time. He needs to be out at sea all day catching fish. A day trying to sell the fish is a day when he's not catching. Also, fishermen are rarely in the business for money. Many of them are after that big fish, the one that their grandkids will talk about for years to come. That's what makes them return to the dangerous ocean day after day.

Just then they spotted my four tunas lying on the deck and an eruption of shouts followed, offering me different values of Pesos, all trying to outbid each other. One of them tried to step onto the boat and Shackleton barked at him, which made him jump back and trip over a large pile of stinking crab pots. It was very funny.

'Right William, it's time to sell your fish.'

'One Pesos, two, three,' were all being shouted at me. Some were even just offering a filleting service in case I wanted to take the fish home and cook it.

'Do we want to keep one Mr Ernie?' I asked.

'Well I think we should. Just the small one there. That should feed us good and proper.'

After a few moments of shouting, I eventually settled on the highest bidder. We agreed on six Pesos for the three big ones and he prepared the smaller one for free. It was all rather exhilarating.

That evening Mr Ernie, who had his own private chef, made us the most wonderful oven baked fish I've ever had, covered in tomatoes and garlic with sweet potatoes on the side. I savoured every mouthful and decided I'd make the same dish for Father on my return.

The week flew by now that Mr Ernie wasn't writing his book. He still wrote something though, every day in the morning before his thinking medicine. Either articles for newspapers and magazines, or personal letters to people who had written to him asking for advice, mostly on how to get their own book published. Mr Ernie simply couldn't reply to everyone, so it became my job to skim through and choose the best three letters each day, to find the people who really seemed to need his advice the most. It was interesting that the people who needed his help the most were also the ones who spent more time on making sure the letter and envelope looked enticing, beautifully written and sealed with a wax stamp. The ones with bad spelling, poor grammar and shoddy handwriting were often the chancers hoping to get a reply. These we often didn't even open.

'You should always take pride in your work Master William,' Ernie would say as he threw a letter written with no love into the bin.

'I know Mr Ernie. My Father says the same.'

'Your Father is a good man.'

'Yes he is,' I said proudly.

By the end of the week, and with two more fishing outings, I was bringing in more than enough to not only get the ship home, but also pay for a return trip to Viñales, and to pay back Mr Ernie for the cost of Shackleton of course.

I think Mr Ernie sensed I had itchy feet, so on the morning of my departure he gave me a small bag.

'In here William, will be some things you may find useful on your adventure. Don't open it now. Don't tell me where you are going, but I'll await a telegram once you've found whatever it is you are looking for, and remember, the ferry comes in twenty days. Don't be late because the monthly ferries thereafter are often delayed due to hurricane season.'

'Ok Mr Ernie.'

'Oh, and one last thing. What do you think I should write my next book about?'

I paused for a moment. There were so many incredible stories in Havana but for me there was only one story.

'I think you should write about the fisherman we saw that first day we went fishing.'

'The old man. Sounds interesting. And what else?' replied Mr Ernie with genuine excitement.

'What do you mean what else?'

'Well sometimes you need to write about two things. You can't just write about the old man.'

'Well, write about the old man and the big wide ocean.

Mr Ernie paused and looked out over Havana from his patio.

'The old man and the sea. I like it Master William. I like it a lot.'

'I think it'll be a very good book Mr Ernie. I can't wait to read it.'

'It shall be my masterpiece. Now keep safe William and make sure you don't do anything that I wouldn't do,' he bellowed.

Shackleton and I walked down his driveway and out onto the main road heading back into Havana. We took a rickshaw taxi into town to the old bank building where our horse and cart was waiting for us. All I could think of was that the Captain had over a week's head start on us.

Chapter 9
The Road Heading West

As Havana slowly disappeared behind us the Cuban countryside opened out. It was hot, frightfully hot as we trundled down old farm tracks past fields of maize and sugarcane. Our first night was in a small town called San Diago de los Banos. Ordinarily this town would have not played any significance in the Cuban countryside, but thirty years previously a wealthy lawyer had built a huge stately home complete with Japanese gardens, ponds and fountains. The grand entrance looked like a medieval castle. I'd never seen anything like it, not even back home. It reminded me of some of the pictures and drawings Father had shown me of castles in Ireland.

'One day Shackleton, we shall have our own castle with a drawbridge and a moat. It'll be the grandest castle in all of the land,' I said and fed him a bit of dried fish.

Shackleton barked in appreciation of my ambition.

But that's when I'm big. For now, we need to stay focused. Captain is far ahead of us. It'll be a miracle if he hasn't found the treasure already.

Later that night at dinner in the local hotel which Shackleton and I could just afford with our tuna sales, we received great news. The Captain had passed here just four days previously, and not the week we had guessed. His convoy of supplies, his team and the overloaded stallions were slow under foot. It had taken him two days to cover what we had in one. Our advantage was our speed and agility. The down side being that we had no supplies and needed to rely on sourcing what we could find. This was easy on a well-trodden trade route to Viñales, but once we headed into the mountains, I'd have to rely on living off the land. This was a concern because the only books I had read on survival were how to survive in Peru, not Cuba. I'd most certainly need to find some books in Viñales to learn about the fruit and berries I could eat, and more importantly, the ones I couldn't. This would put me back a day, but hopefully Captain would rest in Viñales too. After all, he had no idea we were on his tail.

The second day saw us head along the start of the mountain range before cutting north towards Viñales. The hills and heat were tough on the stallions and we were forced to stop every hour to let them rest in the shade and drink some water. Captain's stallions must have had to do the same, but for longer surely.

By late afternoon a lightning and thunder storm engulfed us. Rain was so hard you could barely keep your eyes open and if you dared even talk your mouth soon filled up with water. Shackleton was terrified by the booms and bangs. I've never seen him scared before and it frightened me a little. I forget he too is just like me; a little boy wandering the world looking for answers and trying to figure it all out. The thunderstorm ended as soon as it began. The sun was out again and the rain had cooled things down and the stallions seemed all the better for it.

It was late evening by the time we crested the hill and headed down towards Viñales. The view was breath-taking. The flat valley floor was broken up by 100-metre-high mounds of forested rock. As if a giant had stuck a straw into the earth and blown bubbles out of the ground. In the far distance lay the mountain range. I guessed it to be the one from the map. I desperately wanted to get the map out but didn't want anyone to see it. I got my compass out instead. 'Yes Shackleton,' I shouted in a whisper.
'I think that is the mountain range. That's where we need to head for.'

Shackleton jumped up from hiding under the bench, his beard flowing in the passing air. My focus moved slowly from Shackleton's beard to the mountains in the distance. This was going to be one grand old adventure and I think even Shackleton knew it too.

The plan was to spend one day in Viñales to prepare for my trek into the mountain jungles. I needed to stock up on tinned meat and maybe some rice to boil. I had no pot so I would try and find one too. I wouldn't then need a plate either and could just eat out of the pot. Other than that, I would try and live off the land as much as possible. For this I'd need a book of some sort. Something to learn about how to survive the jungles of Cuba. So far all I knew I could eat were bananas, papaya and coconuts. These seemed to be in abundance near Viñales, however I didn't know if I would find any further into the jungle. That was all for tomorrow, for now I needed a place to sleep. I couldn't afford a hotel so I headed east in search of a cave on the advice from the carriage driver.

It was a mile out of town before I saw the old dead tree signifying the rocky outcrop where the cave was. I climbed up through the prickly thorn bushes and found the small entrance, only big enough for a ten-year-old to crawl through. I stopped, my heart started to race. I didn't know what else may use the cave, a monster snake perhaps. I decided to get a rock and throw it in, but before I had the time to pick one up Shackleton darted from behind me and rushed into the darkness. Suddenly three bats flew out nearly knocking me off my feet. I heard a scurry and then silence.

'Shackleton. Are you OK?' I whispered.

I heard no reply. I waited what seemed an eternity and then suddenly Shackleton was in front of me, his mouth wide open and his tail wagging. He was smiling. I knew it was safe to go inside now. He had made sure of it.

The cave was dark with a nice comfortable soft layer of sand on the ground. It felt like I was at the beach. There was enough sand to even build a mound that I used as a pillow for my weary head.

The next day after the deepest of sleeps we went back into town and I gathered up some supplies. Food, a small pot and some dried fish for Shackleton. I couldn't find a book on living off the land though. This was a huge concern. I enquired in a few shops and said I needed a book about survival as I wanted to explore the jungle, but each and every time the shop keepers laughed and just said 'banditos' and told me that no one goes into the jungle. I guess they thought I was joking. Who were these banditos anyway? I wasn't too worried because I knew adults liked to scare little boys. Like the time the fishermen at the market down by the harbour used to tell me not to go close to the edge of the harbour as there was a big scary monster that would come up from the water and eat me. I knew the real worry was that I'd slip and fall in, and if that happened the Italians may have something to say about it. In any case. I figured this was just another tale to stop kids wandering off alone. And besides, Shackleton was here to look after me.

By midday it was time to head off. Shackleton and I took the smaller paths out of town past what seemed to be tobacco farms. The smell was pretty disgusting. I couldn't understand why adults inhaled this into their lungs. Within a few hours we were all alone heading towards the mountains, and within another few hours we were finally in the heart of the jungle and out of sight. We rested for a while and I poured some water in the palm of my hand for Shackleton to drink. It was very hot, the dense trees shielding us from any sort of breeze that may cool us down. Shackleton always walked in front of me, making sure any snakes, lizards, and spiders moved out the way. We were a good team. It had taken us six hours to do the first five miles. It was slow progress but I guessed still faster than the Captain. At least Shackleton and I could crawl under fallen trees and take shortcuts over small mountains whereas the Captain would have to cut his way through and go around any big obstacles.

By 7pm, as the sun was starting to set, Shackleton suddenly stopped in his tracks.

'What's going on Shackleton?' I whispered.

He looked back at me and then ahead again and gave a low growl. I looked ahead but couldn't see anything. I crouched down and waited for a whole five minutes but still nothing. My knees began to hurt. Surely the thing Shackleton saw would have run away by now. Maybe he just got spooked. I grew impatient.

'Come on Shackleton. We need to make progress. Let's keep going.'

Shackleton barked and blocked me from moving forward.

'Come now Shackleton. It's nothing. We've been here for ages and there's nothing. Maybe it was just the wind,' I said in annoyance.

I pushed past Shackleton and walked about ten metres ahead.

'You see Shackleton, nothing to . . .'

Chapter 10
Banditos?

All of a sudden I was turned upside down. The rush of blood to my eyes temporarily blinding me. I could feel something engulf me, it was prickly and smelled of rotting sweat. I tried to open my eyes but everything was blurry.

'Breathe William, breathe,' I said out loud. Slowly I heard the faint and familiar barks coming from below me.

'Shackleton!' I shouted and he barked back.

My vision was slowly returning too. Shafts of light appeared and then after a few hurried blinks I could finally see. But all I could see, in all directions were tree branches and leaves. Until I looked down and saw Shackleton sitting there barking up at me. I was five metres up in the air.

'The banditos Shackleton. The banditos. Hide. Go and hide Shackleton,' I shouted but he wouldn't move. I knew he wouldn't. I'd never taught him to do that. He just stared up at me and barked.

'Come on Shackleton. Run away. Please,' I pleaded.

Then suddenly I heard Shackleton yelp and fall to the floor. There was a small dart with red feathers sticking out of his leg.

'Shackleton, run boy r. . .'

I couldn't even finish my sentence before I felt a piercing pain in my right calf. I looked down. The same red feathered dart that I saw in Shackleton was now in me. Moments later everything went black and I fell into darkness.

I don't how long I was asleep for, but it must have been a long time because when I awoke the side of my face felt bruised as if I had been lying on it for days. The first thing I thought about was Shackleton. I looked around to see where I was. The room was dark but it was daylight outside. Shafts of light casting lines across the sandy floor. It seemed I was in some sort of hut, a reed hut, with no windows. As my eyes adjusted I tried to see if Shackleton was here, but he wasn't. I was here alone. My mind and thoughts so jumbled I wasn't able to think straight. I started to panic.

'Breathe William. Breathe.'

I took three deep breaths and focused my energy on my surroundings. I heard mumbling coming from outside the hut. I couldn't make out what they were saying but it sounded serious. It lacked the jovial lift in tone at the end of sentences that is usually associated with casual chitchat. I first noticed this when I'd listen to the Italians talk in their native tongue. I was usually allowed in the room when their sentences ended with a higher note, but as soon as this disappeared Father would then often ask me to leave the room. What I heard outside the hut was very similar. Something was going on and I feared Shackleton and I had somehow landed in the middle of it.

I got up slowly and felt a shaft of pain from my calf. I looked down expecting to find a huge hole where I had been stabbed, but was surprised to see a small bandage covering it. There was a tiny red speck in the middle from where my wound had bled while I had been asleep.

I needed to get out of the hut. There seemed to be a door on the same side as where I heard the voices. There was a small gap in the reeds so I moved over, careful not to make any noise. The voices stopped briefly. I froze, holding my breath so as not to make a sound. The voices started up again and I moved close to the hole. I peered through to see out. It was difficult to see through such a tiny hole but I could just about make out five figures sitting around a campfire, one of them a clean-shaven man in his thirties I guess, was smoking a huge cigar, occasionally dipping the bit that goes in your mouth into a tin can. A yellow substance would trickle off the end as he swirled it, put it back in his mouth and continue puffing away. By the way the seats were laid out, it seemed the man with the cigar was the leader. My focus then turned away from the men at the fire to search for Shackleton. I scanned the surrounding from left to right but couldn't see anything. Nothing but jungle, hammocks, and other huts similar to the one that I was in dotted around. This must be one of the bandito base camps that I had been warned about. So the people in Viñales must have been telling the truth.

Suddenly I heard a dog bark and let out a gasp. The man with the cigar looked up with a look in his eyes I've never seen before. It was frightening. He must have heard me. I backed away from the door and went to the far corner. Moments later the door flew open nearly blinding me. I closed my eyes. I felt a hand on my shoulder. A strong hand. I went to cover my face in anticipation of a certain blow to the head. But it did not come. Instead the hand loosened its grip and the man spoke. He had a gentle voice.
'Good afternoon my son.'

He spoke in English but with a Spanish accent. I opened my eyes. It was the leader standing over me. 'Come. You must be hungry. Follow me,' he said and walked back to the door and past the others who were now all looking at me from around the campfire I heard the faint bark again in the distance. 'Shackleton,' I shouted.

The men laughed.

'Come, come. You need to eat,' the leader said again.

I got up slowly and ventured outside to the warm smiles of the others. This was not the bandito camp I had expected. I most certainly would have thought I'd be dead by now.

'My name is Ernesto,' the leader said.

'My name is William Wilder,' I replied.

'William Wilder. I like that. Come eat with us Master Wilder. Like your name, you are now truly in the wild.' How strange I thought that the two people who I had met in Cuba had almost the same name. Ernest and Ernesto. Something in the stars suggested we were meant to meet. This simply couldn't be by chance alone. I heard a bark again. It was definitely familiar. 'Shackleton?'

'Ah, so his name is Shackleton. He has been helping us hunt for rats this morning. He is a natural. You've trained him well,' Mr Ernesto said while dipping his cigar again.

'What's that?' I asked.

'This is the finest honey in all the world William. When I breathe the smoke from my motherland's sacred leaves and mix it with the honey that the bees make, it clears my head and makes me think straight.'

'I knew another man who said the same thing about whisky,' I replied.

All the men burst out laughing.

'Whisky for us makes us sleep William. But everyone has their own ways and who are we to judge. Come now. Eat up. You've been asleep for days.'

Dinner was rat stew that had been simmering on the fire for hours. I wolfed down a huge bowl and a second one shortly after.

Moments later I heard Shackleton barking right behind me. Before I could even turn around I was tackled to the floor, Shackleton jumped all over me and licked my face with excitement. Even though his breath smelled of rat I didn't care. It was so good to see him again.

'So what brings you both into the heart of the jungle?' asked Mr Ernesto.

'Well, Shackleton and I are explorers now.'

All the men listened closely.

'Explorers eh? And what exactly are you exploring for?'

I paused for a moment. Should I tell them, or should I lie? What if they decided to find the treasure themselves? I'd never be able to compete against all of them. They knew this land far better than we did.

'Could it be that you are looking for the sacred caves?' Mr Ernesto winked and held up the page from my notebook with the treasure map on it. He had torn it out. It had the map on one side and the riddle on the other.

'Give it back,' I burst out, and then I felt embarrassed at giving away my motive. I should have pretended to not be bothered by it.

'Don't worry William. The map is yours. We have more important things to do,' said Mr Ernesto in Spanish with a solemn tone. The rest of the men nodded in agreement echoing his sentiment with gruff, 'Si Senor' He walked over and gave me the map.

'But it'll be impossible for you to get to the caves on your own without some basic jungle knowledge.'

'I know, but you see, there is the Captain. He is a few days ahead of me and I need to get there before him. I really do.'

I then told Mr Ernesto and his gang all about the bad potatoes, the Italians and how I needed to get the treasure and the ship back home all in the space of just over a week. Tears began to fill my eyes as I contemplated returning empty handed.

'You see. I just have to succeed, I have to,' I said trying not to show too much emotion. I was a strong explorer after all.

Mr Ernesto who was still standing next to me, smoke from his cigar whirling up into the moonlit evening, put his hand on my shoulder.

'Don't worry, William. We will help you. Now go to bed. You need some rest. Oh, and sorry for the poison arrow in your leg. We thought you were a spy trying to infiltrate us.'

'A spy?' I asked inquisitively.

'What are you doing here?' I continued.

'Well William. You see, we are the revolution. This beautiful island we live on has a very bad leader. We are trying to give it back to the people. We are some years away, but you have somehow managed to stumble across our very first headquarters, deep in the jungle. We may have to rethink where we base ourselves now. If a ten-year-old and his dog can find us, the military certainly will too.'

They all laughed but there was a hint of seriousness to their point. If I could find them, then someone else surely could too.

Mr Ernesto continued to tell me all of their plans, which would still take quite some time and involved them hiding away in the jungle. Mr Ernie did say that if you wanted to hide from the world, this is where you should go.

The main issue as it seemed, was that Mr Ernesto, although a leader, didn't feel he was old and wise enough to be the poster boy for the nation's revolution.

'You see William, I look too young. I am too young actually, but they want me as the figurehead. Not to take over the country, but to be the man who fought for it, because, well... because I guess I have been the driving force. But sometimes you need to look like the person you are trying to be. Even if you are the right person. It's like in a boxing match. A short thin boxer, even though he may be the stronger fighter, will always be considered a lesser boxer than a tall muscular one. Until he proves himself that is. But until that day comes, he cannot rely on just his skill to attract the attention of other fighters. He has to work a lot harder to get to the top.'

I didn't really understand what Mr Ernesto was talking about, but decided I was too tired and would give it more thought in the morning.

'But that is for another day young William. Sleep well and may the treasure gods be in your dreams.'

'Thank you, Mr Ernesto,' I said as my eyes could barely stay open. Shackleton and I wandered back to our hut and were soon fast asleep.

It took two days with Mr Ernesto and his troops learning how to survive the jungle. Spiders that you don't want near your bed at night as they may kill you, and spiders that you do want because they build webs that catch mosquitoes. Mushrooms to eat, mushrooms to use as medicine, and mushrooms to use as poison on the end of your spear. At the end of each day I'd ask if I was ready, but each time Mr Ernesto would simply say;

'Better to have the knowledge and not need it, than need the knowledge and not have it.'

He was a very wise man I thought, but I have to admit that he was right, he didn't look wise at all, not like Mr Ernie for example, who did look wise. I pondered that every day until the last evening while in bed. It came to me.

The next morning while packing up my things and supplies that Mr Ernesto had given me, I told him of my idea.

'Mr Ernesto. I think I know what you need to do to look wiser and gain the support of your country at such a young age.'

'I am listening Master William.'

'I think. .' I paused for a moment, wondering if my idea may just be laughed at but then thought it would be better to say your idea and it not be needed, rather than someone need your idea and you never said it. So I told it.

'I think you need to grow a beard.'

All the troops now gathered around me fell over laughing.

'A beard. Is that all?'

'Yes. I think people with beards seem wiser.'

Mr Ernesto stroked his newly shaven chin.

'You see, if there was a beard there, you could stroke it instead and look wise,' I said.

'Mr Ernesto pondered this and then walked over to his hut. Moments later he came back and told me to put out my hand.

'Here you go master William. Here is my shaving knife. You can have it. You never know. You may need it one day, before you decide to become wise yourself.'

He handed me his bone handled knife.

'Thank you. I don't actually have a knife because Father says they are too dangerous.'

'Well you always need a knife in the jungle. Good luck.'

'Thank you. Oh, and maybe change your name. I've only met two people in Cuba and they both have the same name. Something shorter I think, something different.'

'OK Master William. I shall choose a shorter name to go by.'

'Good!' I said, feeling proud of my involvement with Mr Ernesto's revolution.

'Now Godspeed and remember the good spiders from the bad ones.'

'Thank you,' I said and walked out of the camp heading west. Within metres of leaving the camp it was completely hidden, the only faint hint that anyone was around was the sweet smell of Mr Ernesto's cigar wafting through the jungle.

Chapter 11
The Captain's Secret

Even with the two days with Mr Ernesto, I soon discovered I was only two days behind the Captain. I knew this from how much the cut leaves and branches had wilted from where he had to make his path through the jungle. His progress must be really slow. At this rate it looked like I may catch him tomorrow.

The jungle was a fully stocked pantry once you knew what to look for. Mr Ernesto had taught us well. We lunched on some mushrooms and green leaves for starters, and I gave Shackleton some juicy snails which I fried in my new pot. They smelled like they may taste good but I wasn't quite ready to eat snails just yet. Even the rat I ate with Mr Ernesto now seemed disgusting, but at the time I would have eaten anything.

By early evening the following day Shackleton and I eventually came across where the Captain and his team had decided to camp up for the night. I desperately wanted to get ahead of them, but it was getting too dark and both Shackleton and I were beyond tired, our weary legs tripping over roots more often as our eyes struggled to stay open. As tired as we were I just needed to find out a bit more about the Captain's movements. If he was going to stay here for a few days then that would ease the relentless pressure of making good distance through the dense jungle. I decided it would be a good idea to use my skills from Mr Ernesto and sneak up on them to listen in on their conversations.

'Shhhhh Shackleton. We need to crawl ever so quietly. We can't let them know we're here,' I whispered to Shackleton who for the first time was behind me. We were both crouched low. I was on my hands and knees. I desperately wanted to find out some information, something to keep me in front.

Luckily I knew the campfire glow would make their eyes not accustomed to the dark and I'd be hidden, as long as I stayed in the shadow.

I was ten metres from the fire before I could make out what they were saying.

'Come now Captain. We've got this. We're so close.' One of the men said to him, rubbing his shoulder.

The Captain had his head hung low. It seemed strange to me. The Captain was a strong man, but here he seemed vulnerable.

'We know how much you need it Captain. We will find it.'

The Captain then looked up to the stars and put his hands together as if in prayer.

'God knows if I don't, I'll lose her forever. These operations cost a fortune nowadays.'

Suddenly I could see the look on his face. It looked as if he had been crying.

'Don't worry Captain. You will get that treasure and afford the operation for her. We can be sure of that.'

Suddenly it dawned on me. The Captain had talked about this to Mr Ernie on the ship. His daughter was gravely ill and he said they were waiting on an operation. I had thought it was time they were waiting for, but it looks like it was money they needed. Money in the form of treasure.

Shackleton and I snuck back into the depths of the jungle and set up camp. I felt bad for the Captain but decided there and then what I would do. Shackleton and I would most certainly get to the treasure before the Captain and his crew, and what I'd do is just take enough treasure to help Father and then leave enough for Captain to help his daughter. A huge relief came over me. Suddenly the scary Captain was human and not a monster as my mind had made him out to be. I promised never to judge someone too early and just as Mr Ernie had said, the real story is often not the obvious one.

It took another two days to get to the point where *Treasure Time* was written on the map. Somewhere on this mountain range was a cave with the treasure in it. It wasn't before we were right near its base that we cleared the dense jungle and a towering mountain loomed above us. I looked up and there above me, scattered like spots all over the face of the mountain side, were about 500 small caves, varying in size from three to ten metres in diameter. It could be in any one of these. It would take a month to climb up to every single one of them.

'The riddle Shackleton. The riddle,' I said and turned the page over to read the riddle.

Where treasure lies there are no stairs
High above what comes in pairs

'Something in pairs Shackleton. Look for something in pairs.'

Shackleton barked at something far off to our right. There at the base of the mountain were two palm trees and high above were a series of small caves and one large one.

'There Shackleton. It must be up there.'

We ran over and started to scramble up the mountain. It wasn't too steep to need a rope but I needed to use my hands to grab onto sticks, roots and trees as we made our way up. Within five minutes we came across a big cave. I stopped. The cold air rushing from the cave sent shivers down my spine, I carried on reading the riddle.

The darkest void lies in plain sight
But danger lurks when day turns night

'Not this cave Shackleton. This one is where danger lurks I think.'
We read on.

Dalmatian spots echo before
The whistling birds you must not ignore

'What does that mean?' I asked Shackleton. I looked around.
'Whistling birds?'
I tried to look at every other cave above and around us but I had no idea which direction to go. Shackleton suddenly let out a bark and looked off to the left.
'What is it Shackleton?' I couldn't tell what he was looking at. Then I saw it. The problem was I had been

focusing my energy on each individual cave. I needed to widen my perspective. High above me off to my left were a series of caves, about fifty or so together which made the shape of an animal; a dog.

'Dalmatian Shackleton. Those caves look like a Dalmatian? I shouted and pointed.

Then three little birds swooped down from the sky and darted into one of the caves, their wings rushing through the air making a whistling sound.

'Yes Shackleton. We can't ignore the whistling birds. We are getting close.'

I read on.

If a man does be caught to steal
His digits left, up two, and kneel

I had no idea what this meant. I thought long and hard. What happens if you get caught stealing? Well you get your hand cut off, don't you? Shackleton barked.

'His digits left. Well digits are fingers, so he has five fingers remaining. Left up two, and kneel down,' I continued.

Yes Shackleton. Move five caves to the left of the one with the birds.'

I pointed and counted.

'Then up two caves.'

I counted those and there was the cave we needed to get to.

We spent an hour climbing up to the Dalmatian caves, trying our best not to lose sight of the one we needed to get to. It had a small aloe bush just outside of it and an overhanging rock to its left.

We reached the cave as the sun was setting but to our disappointment it wasn't a real cave at all. It only went about three metres deep.

'What now Shackleton?'

Kneel, it said. So I did. This brought my eyeline below the level of the overhanging rock to the left and there, on the opposite side of another mountain, about two miles away, were three almost identical caves, perfectly in a row about 200 metres apart. With dense jungle below, these caves would have been invisible from the valley floor. You had to get up to these Dalmatian caves to see them. I carried on reading.

Of the three there can only be one
When dusk does glow the wolves become

I had no idea what this meant either. Was I meant to look for a wolf?

The sun was slowly setting. We waited to see if maybe one was a wolf lair or something. Then it started to appear. Very faint at first, but as the sun was just about to dip below the horizon off to our left, a wolf's head started to appear in the shadow of the middle cave. The way the rocks protruded from the side of the cave cast a perfect howling wolf's shadow to the right-hand side of the middle cave. It was as if the wolf was coming out of the cave and letting us know where to go. Then, as soon as it appeared the sun dipped behind a low-lying cloud and then below the horizon and the shadow was gone.

'It's that one Shackleton. The middle one over on that mountain. We must hurry to the middle cave.'

Shackleton barked and sat down. Something was wrong.

'Not the middle cave?'

Shackleton barked. I read the riddle.

It's in the jaws you shall go
And here lies the treasure for all who know

'You are right Shackleton. The open mouth of the wolf's shadow was over the cave to the right. That cave was in the jaws of the wolf's shadow.'

Shackleton jumped up and barked.

'Well done Shackleton. Let's head to the right-hand cave,' I shouted in excitement.

We scrambled down. By the time we reached the bottom it was nearly dark and much too dark to attempt the hazardous climb up to the treasure cave. Mr Ernesto taught me how important it was to sleep off the ground and showed me how to make a hammock out of vines. With a bit of practice, you can get one slung between two trees within the hour. I however took two whole hours to get my vine camping bed up and ready. I laid some leaves on the ground for Shackleton, took out my small blanket and snuggled in for the night. I also put a huge banana leaf over me in case it rained or if a bird pooped on me in the night. Moments later helped by the soothing sounds of the jungle I was fast asleep.

Suddenly I felt something tight around my ankles. I opened my eyes. It was early morning, just enough light to see without needing a torch or candle. I threw the banana leaf off me and looked down. I felt a pull and my leg lifted in the air. It seemed the vine I had used to make my bed was alive and dragging me up into the trees. The grip was painfully tight and I could feel the blood draining from my foot. I remembered Mr Ernesto telling me to beware the shrinking vines. At night they expand and come down to the floor for their hairy bark to absorb nutrients and then in the daytime the vines shrink back up into the trees to avoid being eaten by rats and other animals. My leg was now tangled in the vine and it was slowly pulling me up into the trees. To my dismay Shackleton was still fast asleep. If I stretched down I could just about reach his head. Within minutes though, I'd be out of reach and I'd have to wait till nightfall before I'd be let back down again. Not only was this dangerous, but also it meant the Captain may reach the cave before me and take all the treasure. Then suddenly I thought of something.

'Shackleton! The knife. Get Mr Ernesto's knife from my backpack,' I screamed trying to reach the bag on the floor but my arms just weren't long enough.

Shackleton jumped up immediately and looked up at me.

'Hurry Shackleton. I need the knife now,' I begged, hoping he would understand. He put his head into my backpack and got out a banana.

'No Shackleton, the knife, I need the knife,' I shouted again. He stopped, looked at me, then looked at my ankle being pulled upwards. I was nearly completely upside-down now. He then went into the backpack again and this time, to my amazement, he had the knife in his jaw.

'Good boy. Now bring it here,' I said.

He ran over and I reached down, but at that moment the vine did a sudden jerk upwards. I was now too far out of reach.

'Jump Shackleton, jump. I need you to jump.'

Shackleton immodiately jumped into the air bringing the knife right up to my hands. I grabbed it out of his mouth just before he fell back down.

'Well done my boy,' I said.

I pulled myself up towards my ankle. I needed to cut fast. If I fell now it wasn't too far a fall back onto my hammock, any higher and I'd risk broken bones for sure. I cut the first strand and it went *'twing'* and recoiled up into the trees. I then cut the second one and it too shot upwards. Just a few more to go. One by one I carefully sawed away, making sure I didn't cut my ankle. Finally, the last one went *'snap'* and I fell back down to the hammock, which broke but softened my fall to the floor. Before I could even breathe Shackleton was licking my face.

'That was close,' I said and got up to shake the dirt and leaves off me.

Chapter 12
The Climb

It would be a two hour climb from the jungle up to the cave. It wasn't steep, but the rock sections were slippery so we had to scramble up the sides along the dirt. Up and up we climbed. About halfway up we were high enough to get a view across the valley. About two miles away we saw the dust from Captain's cart heading towards us. Why wasn't he by the Dalmatian caves? Perhaps he'd already worked the riddle out. He had been to Cuba many times before of course. This would mean he'd gain a day on me and was likely to reach the foot of this climb in an hour or so. We needed to move faster.

Shackleton and I pushed hard, grabbing onto roots and trees, my hands blistering and sweat pouring into my eyes from the heat of the morning. I hadn't been looking up much, rather keeping my head down facing the front of the hill when suddenly I bumped my head on a rock above me. I looked up. My heart sank. It was a huge overhang. I looked left and right. The overhang stretched all the way across the mountain. We somehow needed to get up and over this lip. Shackleton came beside me with a bit of vine in his mouth. Yes Shackleton. The vine that nearly took me up into the trees could now be our saviour. I could use it as a rope. I took the vine from Shackleton and pulled as much of it as I needed and then used Mr Ernesto's knife to cut the end off. I then found a medium sized banana-shaped rock that I tied to the end of the rope. This would act as some sort of anchor when I threw it above. I learned a lot about tying rope when I made Larry, so it took me no time at all to get the rock on the end of the vine. I then started to swing it round and round like a windmill. After about ten revolutions I let go and threw it up and onto the ledge above me. I pulled slowly, hoping the stone would get caught on something. I pulled and pulled and the rope suddenly went loose and the rock came crashing down, narrowly missing Shackleton's head. We tried a second time but again the rock didn't catch. I wished I had Larry with me. That would have solved all my problems.

'One more throw Shackleton. One more and then we need to build a ladder,' I said in despair.
Building a ladder would mean going back down to get better wood and then finding thin vine to tie it together with. The Captain would surely overtake me before then and take all the treasure.

I swung and swung to get even more momentum and threw the stone as hard as I could. It flew through the air and went much further over the lip than before. I held my breath and pulled slowly. Wishing on each pull for the rock to stick. Nothing, the vine kept coming. Then right at the last pull I felt the vine tighten. I pulled harder. It tightened even further. I then pulled so hard I managed to lift myself off the ground.

'We've done it Shackleton. It stuck,' I shouted and then realised I needed to keep quiet. My echoes would most certainly be heard far down below in the valley.

'Stay here Shackleton. I need to go up and then find a way of bringing you up after me.'

I began to pull on the rope and put my feet against the cliff. My shoulders still hurt but the strength from carrying Larry around town was working in my favour. It took five minutes before I was able to reach and grab the lip of the overhang and pull myself upward. I rolled onto my belly to look back down. I had already planned in my head on how to get Shackleton up to me. I took my rucksack off and used it as a harness. I tied two ends of the rope to the shoulder straps. I then lowered it down to the bottom until the backpack lay flat on the floor but the straps were still up in the air.

'Walk over the backpack Shackleton. But make sure you go through the straps.'

Instinctively he knew what to do, and once he was over the backpack I pulled it up and It went around his belly. I pulled hard and inch by inch he came up towards me. When he was finally on the ledge with me I looked back to see if I could see the Captain. He was close. I could see his men at the bottom of the mountain preparing for the climb up. They had everything including a ladder. In fact, it looked exactly like Larry. Had he taken Larry from the Tempura? It looked like he had. I needed to go into the cave, fast, find the treasure, and then work out another way to get down so that they wouldn't find me and hold me hostage for it.

I turned around and the opening of the cave lay before me. A cool gentle breeze wafted out, giving me goose bumps all over my body. What lay inside could solve all Father's potato problems. This would be the start to a new and better life where Father didn't have to work for the Italians anymore.

Shackleton went ahead of me and I followed closely behind him. Within metres the cave took a bend to the left and went into complete darkness. I got out my candle and lit it. The floor had fine sand covering it. There were no traces of any footprints before Shackleton's and mine. I could see the anchor footprints I was leaving behind that the Captain had been talking about.

'We must make sure we cover our tracks when we leave Shackleton.'

As the candle flickered, some bats stirred and flew inches from my head. My heart raced. I didn't know what I was looking for. A chest perhaps, full of gold coins and diamonds. I would take half and then leave the rest for the Captain's daughter.

The corridor was long, about 100 metres before it opened out into a huge cavern. I crept in slowly, knowing full well other animals like snakes and rats also liked to live in caves. Where was the chest? I searched left, and then right. Initially I didn't see anything, then something caught my eye on the far wall. It looked like some sort of cave painting with pictures and words. I went closer to inspect it. But just when I was looking up, I tripped on something in the sand and came crashing to the floor in a cloud of dust. It took a few seconds for me to gather myself and for the dust to settle before I saw it. The top of a wooden chest buried in the dirt. I brushed away more sand, my heart was pounding out of my throat. All our worries were about to be over.

Chapter 13
The Big Conundrum

'This is it Shackleton. This must be it,' I said softly. I began to dig around the box. The dirt was soft and came away easily. I reached the latch and was surprised to find it unlocked. I guess if you made such an effort to find the treasure here, a silly lock wouldn't stop you. My heart raced even faster now. I opened the chest slowly. The hinges creaked and more bats went fluttering out of the cave. I opened it even further and peered in but it was too dark. I moved my candle near the opening. A glimmer of gold light reflected back at me.

'It's gold Shackleton. We never have to eat green potatoes ever again.'

I opened the rest of the box and let the lid hit the floor. Another cloud of dust puffed up, completely obstructing my view. I brushed the dust away with my hand as the gold slowly re-emerged. It was magical. What lay before me was the most beautiful golden statue of a Lion holding a shield. Along the bottom it read *'White Lion of Mortimer.'* It was about 30cm high, just small enough to fit in my bag. It looked very valuable. This I would take and leave the rest for the Captain. I put the statue aside and peered back in the chest. There was a velvet blanket below where the statue had laid. I whipped it off to see what was below it. My heart sank. Nothing. There was nothing else In Ihc chest at all.

'There must be other chests,' I said and got up For ten minutes I searched high and low all over the cave but found nothing. Outside I could hear the Captain and his men nearing the overhang. I went and sat down next to the gold statue. What a predicament I was in. I could either take the statue and Father would be free from the Italians while the Captain's daughter would remain very ill or even worse - which wasn't worth thinking about. Or I could leave it for the Captain to save his daughter, and we would have to keep eating the green potatoes and working with the scary Italians. As I pondered the terrible situation I was in, my focus turned to the cave paintings. Strangely the words were written in English, something I hadn't noticed in desperation to find the treasure.
It read;

Begin with the words: Tempura lets go
While from the lips you shall blow
Hold it close and never fear
Whisper a place and time so it can hear

Then split the rock along its half
So it can show you the rightful path
Press the compass buried in the centre
To start the journey, you then must enter

Another riddle. I wasn't in the mood for a riddle. My gaze moved over to the drawing next to the riddle. It looked like a pyramid of circles with the three top circles having a wavy emerald green line through them. They looked almost exactly like the rock I had found on the *Tempura*. Wait. Maybe the drawings weren't circles, but in fact a pile of rocks and the top three rocks were like the one I had in my bag. I opened my rucksack and ferried down to the bottom to find the rock. I brought it out and compared it to the cave painting. It was identical in shape and size. Maybe the riddle and the rocks were linked somehow. I decided to test it. I held the rock in my hand and began the phrase.

'Tempura lets go,' I whispered.

I then held the rock up toward the ceiling of the cave and blew on it. The riddle then said I needed to whisper a place and time. Well I've always wanted to go to Peru. I held the rock up again.

'I'd like to go to Peru today please,' I whispered.

But nothing happened. Sweat was pouring down my face. I could hear the Captain and his crew had just reached the bottom of the ledge.

Wait. The riddle said 'Bring it close . . .'

I brought the rock up to my face and whispered again.

'I'd like to go to Peru today please.'

Still noting happened. Maybe I needed to make it simpler for the rock to understand. I brought the rock right up to my lips.

'Peru. Today,' I said softly again.

The green line suddenly went bright. It sparkled a million times brighter and more beautiful than even the gold. I became entranced by it. I continued with the riddle and split the rock in half. The top half came off. In the centre of the bottom half was a compass, just like the riddle said. My heart was racing. I could now hear the Captain at the entrance to the cave. I pressed the centre of the compass and immediately in front of me a small brilliant green puddle formed. It was about a meter wide and shimmering. I got up and looked inside. There to my utter astonishment I could see a satellite view of Peru from above. I stumbled back and tripped over the chest and dropped the rock. Like a magnet they snapped back together again and the puddle disappeared. As I sat there I realised *Treasure Time* on the map wasn't for the gold at all. It was for this. This was the real treasure. The gold was no longer important for I had found something far more valuable to me. I had in my possession, a time machine.

The End

The next book . . .

The Adventures of Norah Knight
The Kalahari Queen

Norah Knight is the daughter of a ship's Captain. She has been very ill for quite a long time but eventually her father returns from an expedition to find treasure with enough gold to pay for her operation that will make her better again. He tells her of a boy called William Wilder who actually found the treasure first but for some reason decided not to take it and simply disappeared unexplainedly through a hole in the ground.

Norah Knight and Haru, her pet falcon, are determined to find William Wilder to find out what happened to him.

Printed in Great Britain
by Amazon